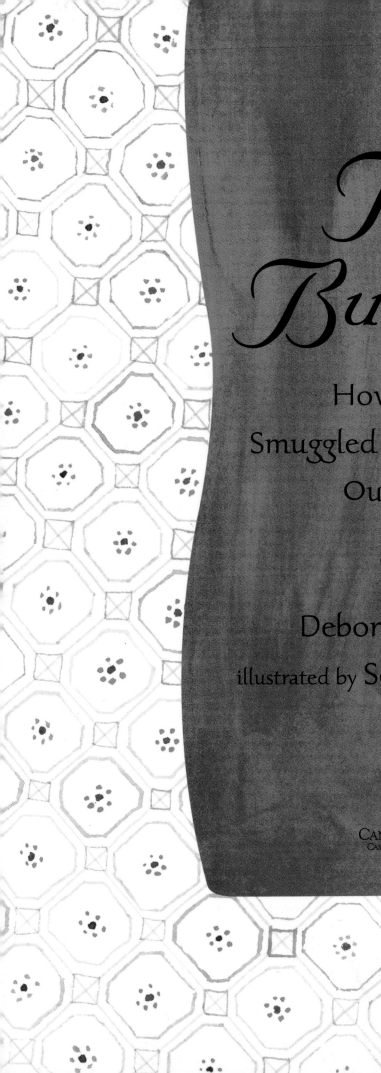

Red Butterfly

How a Princess
Smuggled the Secret of Silk
Out of China

Deborah Noyes

illustrated by Sophie Blackall

CANDLEWICK PRESS
CAMBRIDGE, MASSACHUSETTS

In my father's kingdom
there are many splendors.
Bells and drums and conchs
sound in the city streets.
All day long, ladies
with careful eyebrows
crisscross palace courtyards.
Warlords and courtiers come
and go in gleaming carriages.

In my night chamber

I remove silver pins,

and my hair spills into

my gentle maidservant's hands.

I watch the bright moon

and breathe the breath

of peach petals on the wind.

I am a child with my hair

yet cut across my forehead,

but soon I will marry

the king of far Khotan.

"The moon will follow you

to Khotan," my maid croons,

combing my black hair back.

"The moon will remember."

Good-bye, pink peach petals.
Good-bye, yellow moon.

In my father's kingdom
there are many splendors.

Most valued of all is silk.

Faraway rulers wish for China's

wealth and call it

woven wind.

Silk, my red butterfly wings flapping,

is our people's solemn secret,

thousands of moons old,

spun by a little worm that feeds

on the mulberry leaves

in Father's gardens.

While I walk,

it whispers,

whispers.

The night before

we journey

to the summer palace,

Mother and her maids

drape me in swirls of silk.

The seamstress clips and

stitches, snips and tucks.

Mother whispers that

when the wild geese fly

and the court ladies swap their robes

for squirrel-skin coats, I will go

with those geese:

"You must be brave,

little Daughter."

Good-bye,
   small silkworm.
Good-bye,
   red butterfly.

In my father's kingdom
there are many splendors.
As we cross the wide countryside
to the summer palace,
sunbeams slice through dark woods,
spilling on moss. Monkeys wail
in maple groves along the river.
Sparrows peck mud
for their nests.

When we arrive,

Mother and the other consorts

bathe in the palace hot springs.

After, in belted robes

and wide sleeves,

they look like loveliest butterflies.

The night court hums with poets.

Scroll painters stretch white silk.

Men stand with crossed arms,

topknots bobbing,

to watch the dancers,

while ladies twitter

in pearl-studded gowns.

I sip from my bowl of tea

as my favorite singer tunes

her *pipa: pluck* and *snap*

and *plang,* like rain on rooftops.

When Father returns

from the morning hunt,

I dare not look at him, though

I let my pleadings soar: "But Father,

is not Khotan very far in the dry,

hot desert?"

"Your bridegroom rules a green oasis

in the sand, my daughter.

Grapes sag on the vine, and rivers flow

from the Kunlun Mountains.

Camels and caravans pass to the west

bearing bright goods."

"I do not wish to leave

your honored home."

I swipe at a tear, stooped under

the emperor's gaze, rustling

in red silk,

        rustling.

Good-bye, *pipa* song.
Good-bye, sparrows
pecking at mud.

In my father's kingdom
there are many splendors,

but on the night we return to the

walled city,

my littlest brother,

a shadow behind the screen,

plays for me his simple flute,

made from the bone

of a red-crowned crane.

The notes float,

and I stand by the window,

remembering cranes under the pines,

snowy blossoms of sour plums,

mallow flowers, autumn moons.

What if I pass the mountains and

there is only sand

forever more?

I would give every silver hairpin,

every jade carving and gold ornament

for one brush of southern mist,

one windy, silken promise—

   that home be with me always.

Good-bye,
      red-crowned crane.
Good-bye, sour plums.

In my father's kingdom
there are many splendors.

Will it matter so much if I take just

one away with me to far Khotan?

My maidservant lowers her eyes.

"It is a crime."

Yet when the wild geese call,

she twists and rolls and pins hair

like black silk high upon my head.

She weaves within, like secrets

on the wind, tiny worms spinning

their busy homes.

We hide also the seeds

of the mulberry tree.

We plant them in the soil of me.

"The moon will remember."

She kisses my forehead.

"Now go, and be a queen."

Good-bye, princess.

With my sedan chair ringed

by matchmakers and lantern bearers,

I pray to the gods

and our honorable ancestors.

Father and Mother smile,

but their smiles

dazzle like the sun,

and I look away.

If you must go,

with your hair yet cut

across your forehead,

from all you know,

take with you

some small piece

of brightness,

some shining memory,

for the world is large,

little butterfly,

and the road is long.

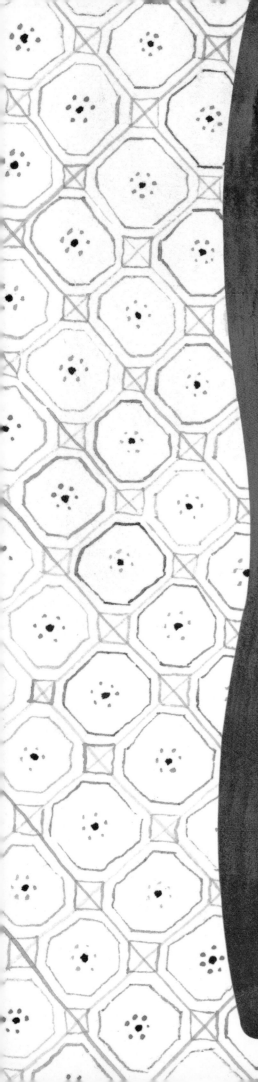

Author's Note

According to Chinese legend, silk was discovered almost five thousand years ago by Si Ling-chi, the young wife of the mythical Yellow Emperor, Shi Huangdi. Strolling in the garden one day, the empress plucked a cocoon of the silkworm moth *(Bombyx mori)* from a mulberry tree. When she accidentally dropped the cocoon into her bowl of tea, she saw a soft but sturdy fiber unravel. Si Ling-chi—known in legend as the Goddess of Silk—is credited both with introducing the silk-making process and with inventing the loom, though recent archaeological finds show the origins of sericulture, the making of silk and silk fabric, to be much earlier.

The Silk Road, a four-thousand-mile-long network of roads or caravan routes skirting forbidding deserts and mountain ranges, officially opened about 200 BC. From around 500 BC to AD 1500, this route served as the major highway for the transport of goods and knowledge between Europe, the Near East, India, and China. A wealth of exotic and commercial goods—from jade, paper, and spices to horses, coral, and grapes— were exchanged, while at the same time skills,

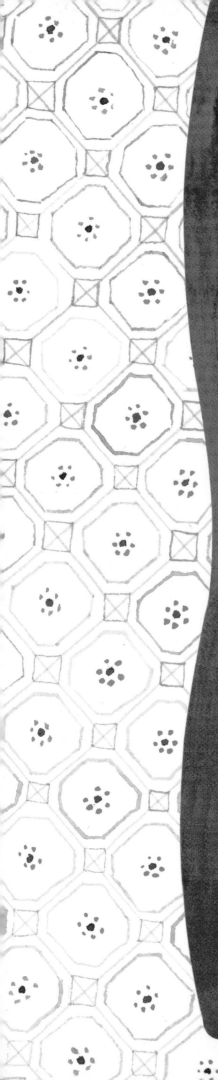

knowledge, and religion (notably Buddhism) crisscrossed the Eurasian continent. But the major product being traded from east to west on this route, as the name suggests, was silk, and the Chinese fiercely guarded the secret of its production. This secret may be one of the most protected and most coveted in history. The punishment for revealing it was death.

It is said that somewhere between AD 100 and 500 (sources vary), a Chinese princess married the king of Khotan, an oasis north of the Plain of Tibet. When she left her native land to travel west to her bridegroom, the princess carried—smuggled in her fancy hairdo or headdress—silkworm cocoons and the seeds of the mulberry tree on which the little worms feed.

Khotan too seems to have guarded the secret, but around AD 550 two industrious monks arrived at the emperor Justinian's court with live silkworm eggs hidden in hollow bamboo walking sticks. The Byzantine Empire soon became a center of silk production in its own right, and sericulture gradually spread throughout western Asia and Europe.

For Aidan and Lisa Bowe—who wanted a story about silk
D. N.

To my mother, for everything
S. B.

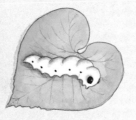

Text copyright © 2007 by Deborah Noyes
Illustrations copyright © 2007 by Sophie Blackall

First edition 2007

Library of Congress Cataloging-in-Publication Data

Noyes, Deborah.
Red butterfly : how a princess smuggled the secret of silk out of China /
Deborah Noyes ; illustrated by Sophie Blackall. –1st ed.
p.   cm.
Summary: In long-ago China as a young princess prepares to leave her parents' kingdom
to travel to far-off Khotan, where she is to marry the king,
she decides to surreptitiously take with her a precious reminder of home.
ISBN 978-0-7636-2400-2
[1. Princesses—Fiction. 2. Silkworms—Fiction. 3. China—Fiction.]
I. Blackall, Sophie, ill. II. Title. III.
Title: How a princess smuggled the secret of silk out of China.
PZ7.N96157Red 2007
[Fic]–dc22   2006052931

2 4 6 8 10 9 7 5 3 1

Printed in China

This book was typeset in Oxalis.
The illustrations were done in Chinese ink and watercolor.

Candlewick Press
2067 Massachusetts Avenue
Cambridge, Massachusetts 02140

visit us at www.candlewick.com